Found Dogs

Erica Sirotich

CITY SHELTER

Dial Books for Young Readers

1 dog,

long and low.

2
dogs,

silver and slow.

3
dogs,

quivering, shivering.

4 dogs,

dressed for snow.

5 dogs,

wimpery, whiney.

6 dogs,

spotty, shiny.

7 dogs,

quick and slick.

8 dogs,

teeny-tiny.

9 dogs,

wrinkled and round.

10 dogs,

slobbering hounds.

Wait, dogs,

a little longer . . .

Soon, dogs,

you'll be found!

10 dogs,

saying hello.

9 dogs,

ready to go.

8 dogs,

stealing kisses.

7 dogs,

snuggling so.

6 dogs,

meet and greet.

5 dogs,

smiling sweet.

4 dogs,

wagging tails.

3 dogs,

dancing feet.

2 dogs,

ready to play.

1 dog,

on her way.

These patient pound dogs . . .

Now they're family!

Found dogs.

FOR RUSSELL
REDFUR ♡

Dial Books for Young Readers
Penguin Young Readers Group
An imprint of Penguin Random House LLC
375 Hudson Street
New York, NY 10014

Copyright © 2017 by Erica Sirotich

Library of Congress Cataloging-in-Publication Data

Names: Sirotich, Erica, author, illustrator.
Title: Found dogs / Erica Sirotich.
Description: New York, NY : Dial Books, 2017. | Summary: "Counts up ten dogs
who are waiting in a shelter, then counts back down to one as each dog is
adopted"—Provided by publisher.
Identifiers: LCCN 2016028517 | ISBN 9780399186417 (hardback)
Subjects: | CYAC: Stories in rhyme. | Dogs—Fiction. | Animal
shelters—Fiction. | Counting. | BISAC: JUVENILE FICTION / Concepts /
Counting & Numbers. | JUVENILE FICTION / Animals / Dogs. | JUVENILE
FICTION / Animals / Pets.
Classification: LCC PZ8.3.S61744 Fou 2017 | DDC [E]—dc23 LC record
available at https://lccn.loc.gov/2016028517

Manufactured in China on acid-free paper
1 3 5 7 9 10 8 6 4 2

Designed by Mina Chung • Text set in Chalkboard
The art in this book was created in ink, using brushes and pens;
it was then composed and colored digitally.